FRANCIS LEGGETT

BANSHEE
IN THE
BASEMENT

TALES OF DARK WONDER
BANSHEE IN THE BASEMENT
©2017 Francis Leggett
First Edition
Edited by Christina Hargis Smith
Cover art by Jeffrey Kosh Graphics
Published by Optimus Maximus Publishing, LLC

ISBN-10: 1-944732-31-4
ISBN-13: 978-1-944732-31-8

To my amazing fiancée, Kirsty for not only putting up with my unintentional ignorance throughout the writing period, but going above and beyond in supporting it.

Iain

Thanks for the support!

Francis Legge

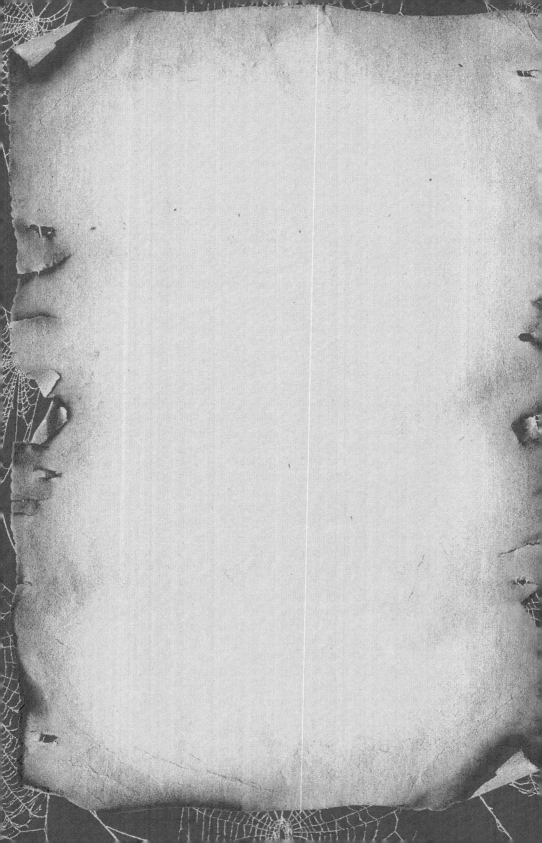

Acknowledgements

I would like to show my gratitude to the following individuals, each have played an important part in making this a reality. Should this book be a success, it is in no small way because of them.

Leon Brown for allowing me to consistently bounce both good and bad ideas off him, and for his unwavering confidence in me throughout.

Christina Hargis Smith for putting her faith, time and hard work into a lad from England with big dreams of becoming an author.

Jeffrey Kosh for his incredible work on the graphics, he has the uncanny ability to pick the images from my mind and bring them to life.

And of course, Lachlan Smith, Alana Stewart, Lily Butler and Samantha Hay for being the first kids to read this book and for all of the amazing ideas they gave me along the way.

ONE

ONE

"To control the night, what a peculiar gift that would be," Danny Banks whispered to himself, pulling his time-worn blankets up to his chin in a vague effort to create a cocoon of heat within his freezing cold bedroom. He flinched at the harsh caress of the covers and vigorously rubbed his freckled face. He hated his old bed sheets; they were patterned with holes and stains, with a texture so rough they made him itch all over.

Trying to ignore his discomfort for yet another night, he turned his focus to the glowing moonlight, beaming in through cobweb coated windows. He had always found comfort in the night's guardian, almost considering it a friend, his only friend actually. It delivered warmth within him that he had not witnessed in a very long time; he knew that whilst the moon stood guard over him with its piercing gaze, he would always be safe.

Danny's fantasy was sharply interrupted by his bedroom door creaking open. He slinked down the bed, covering his face, leaving only a nest of curly brown hair in the open. What could it be? he wondered. A burglar? A monster? The more he thought about it, the more he became frozen with fear.

A gentle tugging triggered his curiosity and he slowly peered out from his linen shelter, revealing his light brown eyes, wide with fear. Slowly turning his head toward the doorway, his eyes met the jade green stare of his Aunt's cat, Merelda, as she pawed at his bed.

"Up here, Kitty,"

With a huge sigh of relief, Danny patted his bed, three times in swift succession, inviting the cat to join him. She was keen to accept the invitation and with a shake of her tail, leapt onto the bed. He ran his hand along the full length of Merelda; she was a long and slender creature with sleek, black fur, soft to the touch. Though he didn't usually like cats, he was glad of some companionship.

"I wish my parents would come back for me," he explained to the purring cat, which was now sprawled across the bed, leaving Danny curled up in a ball on a small corner of the lumpy mattress.

"I'm only ten. My parents wouldn't leave me here forever, they'll be back for me soon, I know it," Danny said, almost trying to persuade himself.

Life had been pretty normal up until four weeks ago, he thought. I had plenty of friends, a family who loved me and Baggles the sheepdog.

Oh, how he missed his Baggles. They used to do everything together, from running in the park to playing detectives, investigating abandoned buildings, but that all stopped four weeks ago, when his mother ran away and left him with his Aunt Agnes. She promised they would only be visiting for the weekend, three days at most, but alas, here he was, still stuck in this cold and creepy house with only a cat for company.

He nestled his head into his thin pillow and drifted into a fitful sleep, his mind feasting upon memories of his mother and Baggles.

What seemed like only seconds later, Danny's dreams were penetrated by a persistent banging. At first the noises were part of a dream he was having, but soon the images melted away and his eyes slowly blinked open. His first reaction was to feel blindly around the bed for Merelda, who had up and left the room as soon as the attention had stopped. The sunlight beaming through the window quickly told him that it was morning.

As the incessant noise continued, Danny sat upright. What is that? He mused, letting out a groan and shuffling to the edge of his bed. Rubbing his face, he slowly rose to his feet and clambered over to the window, brushing aside the cobwebs, to create a small porthole to peer through. His sight was slow to focus so he shook his head in an attempt to hasten the process. When his vision finally adjusted to the light, he looked across the street to see an old man hammering a wooden sign into his front lawn. Danny squinted, trying to make out the writing on the sign, but it was just a blur. He tried to open the window in order to get closer but the handle was stuck.

"Stupid window probably hasn't been opened in a hundred years," Danny grunted in frustration.

Sulking back over to his bed, his foot caught in something and he stumbled to the floor in a crumpled heap.

"What's all the noise up there? Can't I get some peace in my own house? Don't make me come in there," the shrill voice of his aunt echoed throughout the old house. Danny filled with a familiar dread, the colour draining from his face.

"Yes, Aunt Agnes. I'm fine. Thanks for asking," Danny whispered sarcastically, picking himself up from the floor and brushing the dust from his clothes. He went to take another step but he was still caught up in a tangle. Looking down he noticed the strap from a pair of old binoculars wrapped around his ankle. Bending down, he groaned, maybe he hit the ground harder than he had thought. He freed himself from the strap and picked up the binoculars. Looking through them he noticed they were cracked making it impossible to see through the right side. He sat down and rubbed his eyes, the broken lens made him feel dizzy.

"What use is a pair of broken binoculars?" he mumbled to himself. It wasn't until he looked at the window again that a plan hatched itself in his mind. He could use the binoculars to read the sign. Why didn't he think of it earlier?

Danny staggered back over to the window, his knees bruised from the fall. He held the binoculars to his face, pretending he was a hero with super vision. Looking around for the sign he stopped suddenly as he focussed on a patch of green tartan. He slowly moved his view upward and jumped back as he was met by the scowling face of the old man from across the street. Moving the binoculars away from his face, he recovered his composure enough to make eye contact with the old man. He was bald, with skin like leather, and a bulbous, red nose that dominated his grumpy face.

Danny jumped back once more as the old man pointed a long bony finger in his direction. "You, read," the old man mouthed dramatically to ensure Danny could read his lips. The long bony finger changed direction and began to slowly tap the top of the recently erected sign. Danny quickly stepped back over to the window aiming the binoculars at the sign.

He nodded quickly at the old man to confirm that he had read and understood, although really he was still trying to make sense of it all.

He slowly turned away from the window, his distracted mind forgetting to remove the field glasses from his face. Danny let out a sudden shriek and dropped them to the floor as his vision was filled by an enormous figure, silhouetted in the doorway of his room...

TWO

The binoculars hit the floor with a deafening clatter. Danny stood, motionless, eyes wide, staring his fate in the eye.

"Do you mind? Those were my husband's. If you break them, you'll pay, you little nuisance," Aunt Agnes threatened, shuffling further into the room from the doorway.

Danny wanted to back away as she came closer to him but he was so afraid, it was as though his feet had grown into the floor.

Aunt Agnes shambled toward the window and stared knowingly at the peep hole, he had created. He swallowed hard, the anticipation of her next move weighing heavy on his shoulders. She turned around and glared at him, her beady eyes, two black holes in the middle of her gaunt face. She had an uncanny ability to make Danny feel about three inches tall.

"You've been staring out of the window again haven't you?" she probed.

Danny's words were caught in his throat as it tensed up.

"Answer me, boy. You've been spying on the

neighbours again, haven't you?"

"I-I-I-" Danny stammered.

"I know you have so there's no point in trying to deny it. What did I tell you about spying?"

"That the outside world is bad enough, without introducing a wretched little pest like me into it," Danny recited from the hundreds of times she had said it to him.

"That's right, nuisance, don't you forget it." Aunt Agnes spat out her words with such venom. Making her way slowly back to the doorway, she turned to face him once more, her ancient neck creaking in protest. "Your chores won't do themselves, boy. If I'm stuck with you, you'll do as I say. Get to it,"

Danny was so sick of being a slave to his Aunt Agnes. He missed his mum, he missed Baggles, but what could he do? He was just a boy as his aunt regularly reminded him.

Feeling defeated, he slunk down the stairs, trying not to attract any attention to himself. He often forgot how large his aunt's house was, due to spending most of his time confined to his cramped bedroom. He regularly asked if he could sleep in the more spacious guest room instead but was always met with the same response.

"And what do you expect me to do if somebody important wants to stay?" She would grin at him slyly, her facial hair curling into her mouth.

He tiptoed past the living room, where his aunt spent most of her time, and was relieved when there was no piercing scream, aimed in his direction. Confidently, he strode into the kitchen, but he was stopped in his tracks as his Aunt Agnes stood before him, the scowl on her face, framed by her grey mane.

Legs trembling, he struggled to keep his footing. His stomach felt as though it were home to a thousand butterflies. How did she get here so quickly? What can I do? he thought, scanning the kitchen for a safe escape route, but it was too late.

"Hi, Aunt Agnes." He tried a light hearted approach, in the hope that it would diffuse her anger.

"Don't you speak to me as though you're my equal, boy. Have you no manners, you little runt?"

Grabbing him by the shirt, she dragged him toward the sink. Peering over, he noticed it was filled with dirty crockery.

"I told you an hour ago that you had chores to do."

Danny knew it had only been ten minutes since she gave him his orders, but he also knew that it was never worth arguing with her. It only made things worse.

"I'm sorry, Aunt Agnes." He hung his head, not out of shame, but to avoid making eye contact with her.

"Sorry? What is sorry? Sorry won't get me my wasted time back, will it?" she seethed. "When I tell you to do something, you do it. Not in a minute, not in an hour. I demand an instant response, is that clear?"

Danny nodded rapidly, wishing with every fibre of his being that his aunt would leave the room.

"What's the matter, boy? Lost your voice? Cat got your tongue?" Aunt Agnes burst into a throaty cackle and shuffled toward the door.

Danny didn't understand what was so funny; he was just relieved that she was leaving. He gently pulled up a small stool and clambered onto it in order to reach the sink and do his chores. He'd always been a small boy. His mum always told him that the best things come in small packages. These days, however, he was most accustomed to being called a useless runt.

After the washing up, he was expected to vacuum, tidy up, and dust every flat surface in the house. Placing the last clean plate back into the cupboard, Danny put away the stool and made his way out of the kitchen, arms aching from washing every dish in the house. Once again, he tiptoed past the front room, so as not to disturb his aunt, but was relieved to hear her snoring as he passed by.

He opened the nearby storage cupboard and was about to grab a cloth when he heard some commotion from outside. He knew that if he opened the front door, his aunt would wake up instantly and take great delight in punishing him for daring to step outside. Instead, he ran upstairs as fast as his legs would carry him and into his bedroom.

Picking up the binoculars from the floor, he stared out of the window, looking for any signs of a disturbance. It didn't take him long to notice a silhouette in the upstairs window across the street. Though the curtains were drawn, the figure resembled the old man he'd seen earlier. His arms were flailing wildly and Danny could hear him screaming and yelling at the top of his voice. Who is he yelling at? Is he in danger? Danny wondered, desperately wishing he could hear what was being said. He squinted his eyes, as though that would somehow help him see through the curtains. Frustrated, he lowered the binoculars. As he did, a second figure, tall and slender, appeared beyond the window and reached out for the old man. Danny quickly put the binoculars to his eyes again, not wanting to miss a thing. It took him only a few seconds to find the window in his line of vision but as his eyes focussed, he came to the stark realisation that one of the silhouettes was gone.

"Where did the other one go? I only looked away for a second." His eyes widened, trying desperately to make sense of what he'd just witnessed.

Suddenly, the curtains were thrown open and the menacing face of the old man stared back at him.

THREE

THREE

Danny spent the rest of the day haunted by images of the snarling old man. Why was he so scared? He was once such a confident and outgoing young boy. Unfortunately, since his mother had left him under the glaring eyes of his aunt, he'd felt his personality slowly drain away. Baggles was always a safety blanket of sorts too. When he was with him, he felt invincible. Without his trusty dog or his mother, he was afraid of his own shadow.

There was a troubling question, weighing heavy on Danny's mind. He knew he needed to tell somebody what he'd witnessed, but his aunt was the only person he could talk to. He decided that he would burst if he didn't tell somebody soon. Releasing a calming sigh, he made his way slowly down the wide staircase, trying not to disturb Aunt Agnes and send her into another fit of rage. The final stair creaked beneath his foot, a groan escaping from the woodwork. Danny cringed as he heard his aunt get up from her favourite chair.

"Is that you, boy?" she questioned.

"Yes, Aunt Agnes, I wanted to speak to you for a moment," he said, choosing his words carefully.

"Talk to me, boy?" Aunt Agnes looked

surprised.

"Yes, please. I saw something and I can't get it out of my mind," he admitted, eyes filled with the horror that he'd witnessed.

"Fine, fine. You've got sixty seconds, so I advise you don't stop for breath," she mocked.

Danny inhaled slowly before daring to relive that terrifying moment. "I heard shouting from outside so I ran up to my room and looked out of the window to see what was happening. Then I saw the old man across the road, he was shouting and arguing with someone, or something. I picked up my binoculars, so I could see better and when I looked again, one of them was gone and the old man was staring at me." His voice shook with fear. However he couldn't decide if it were fear of what he'd seen, or anticipation of his aunt's reaction. Looking up at her, he noticed her eyes were bulging and a vein pulsated in the middle of her forehead. She released a large sigh and glared at him.

"So, let me get this clear, boy. What you're telling me is, you were spying on the neighbours again?"

"Well-"

"I don't want to hear another word from you, nuisance," she spat, shuffling closer to him, the dominant smell of extra strong skin cream emanating from her wrinkled stockings. "You're just like you're mother. She was an annoyance, and ignorant like you,"

"My mum was not-" Danny caught his tongue before he said something he'd regret.

"How dare you answer me back? Who do you think you are? You are nobody, a nothing, a waste of skin. Go to your room and stay there. I'd better not see your face again until tomorrow,"

Danny was so angry it felt as though his blood was boiling. He turned and stormed up the stairs and into his bedroom, slamming the door behind him. He crumpled to the floor, his back against the wall, his head resting on his knees. Tears began to stream down his face as he sobbed quietly, not wanting to give his aunt the satisfaction of knowing she'd upset him.

Taking a deep breath, he tried to regain his composure, though he could control the sobbing, the river of tears continued to roll down his red cheeks. He had never felt so helpless and alone. Feeling drained of all energy; he crawled onto his bed and found a space to lie between the lumps on his mattress. Wiping away his tears, he reached a soggy hand under his pillow and pulled out a frame and a notebook. It was old and worn, he'd found it on his first evening in the house whilst he was doing his many chores. Deciding it would be good to record his thoughts on paper; he sneakily slid it into the waistband of his trousers and hit it under his shirt.

Placing the book to the side, he revealed an old wooden frame. Within the glass centre a picture was housed, and etched in an eternal memory upon it was a very young Danny, cradled in the loving arms of his mother, her face alight with pride.

An involuntary sigh escaped from Danny as he thought of so many fond memories of his mother and he laughing and playing. How could she love him so unconditionally and yet, leave him with such a disgusting human being? The question had bugged him for weeks, yet he was still no closer to an answer.

He placed the frame safely back under his pillow and stretched over for the notepad, struggling to reach it he picked it up between two finger tips and dragged it closer. Slipping out of his precarious grip it fell open in front of him at the first page, an entry from four weeks earlier.

'Dear Diary, I don't usually do this, but I fear you may be my only friend, for a while. Today, my

life changed dramatically, and not for the better. This was supposed to be a fun, bonding weekend for me and mum. She'd been working a lot lately and wanted us to spend some time together. I'd never heard of my Aunt Agnes before this weekend, and a big part of me wishes I never had. Mum described her to me as a lovely, caring old lady who just needed some company to stop her from being lonely. I was honest with her and told her that I didn't want to spend the weekend with an old woman I didn't know

"Come on, now, Tum-Tum. I'll be with you the whole time. Everything will be, just fine," she'd reassured me. I still felt nervous about the whole thing, but I always felt safe when she called me Tum-Tum. It was a pet name she'd given to me the day that I was born. She'd actually referred to me as Tum-Tum, before calling me Daniel. Apparently the pet name was given to me because I was born with a mild skin condition that left my tummy glowing bright red compared to the rest of my body, but I'm getting off topic.

We arrived outside of the large, grey house. It stood out compared to the rest of the street as the only one that had not been modernised. It looked as though the slightest gust of wind would cause it to crumble. As I climbed the few steps leading to the large double doors, I noticed a huge stone gargoyle towering over me. Once again I told my mum that I wasn't comfortable here but she'd reassured me once more. Mum reached up and with a creak and a thud, used the old fashioned door knocker. Seconds later, Aunt Agnes' voice tore through the silence.

"Yes? Who's there?" she'd asked, innocently.

"It's, Carolyn and your nephew, Danny," Mum replied, cheerily.

The door swung open and in the doorway, stood my Aunt Agnes, beady eyes looking me up and down.

"Yes, he'll do nicely," she'd said without thinking. "I mean, he'll be a great help over the weekend. Won't you, young man?" she corrected herself.

Mum smiled and gently guided me into the house; my heart was pounding in my chest. I wasn't sure if it was due to nerves or all the dust in the air that I was inhaling. Either way, I was far from comfortable, and come to think of it, I haven't been since.

Aunt Agnes shambled into the living room, followed closely by mum. Before I could enter the room, Aunt Agnes had turned to me.

"Go up the stairs, turn left and the last door on your right is your room, from now on."

From now on? I still don't understand what she meant by that.

"Go and unpack your things, there's a-"Aunt Agnes closed her eyes and swallowed hard. It was as though her stomach was tying itself in a knot. "There's a good boy." She shook her head and continued to shuffle into the living room.

My suitcase was too heavy to lift with one arm so I gripped it with both hands and dragged it carefully behind me, one step at a time. I was relieved when I made it to the top without falling down. Looking around I noticed a corridor that seemed to go on forever, with door after door on either side.

"Turn left, last on the right," I recited to myself over and over until I was stood in front of my new bedroom.

I pushed the door open and took my first step inside expecting yet another huge room but was surprised to see it was not much bigger than a shoe box. This place made me nervous, so I dumped my suitcase down in an explosion of dust and hurried back downstairs, to my mum. Running into the living room, my foot caught on the uneven carpet and I went crashing to the ground.

"What do you think you're doing, you clumsy fool?" Aunt Agnes shrieked, her angry face, a picture of horror.

I slowly sat up, rubbing my throbbing knee.

"Mum, I've hurt my-" I looked around the living room and noticed; only my Aunt was there. My mum was gone...

FOUR

Danny threw down his diary, the frustration he felt beginning to peak. He remembered asking his aunt where his mum was, but he always got the same reply.

"She dumped you on me and ran away. The most sensible thing that fool ever did, if you ask me." The words echoed within him. Danny constantly battled the possibility in his mind. He didn't want to believe that his mother would run away and leave him.

Calming down, he placed the photograph and diary back under his pillow. He slumped down in the bed, the lumpy mattress pushing into his ribs. Staring at the ceiling, his eyes felt heavy. The soothing rhythm of the rain hitting his bedroom window gave him something to focus on rather than his own thoughts. The moon was nowhere to be seen; unfortunately it was hidden by a blanket of black clouds.

Suddenly, Danny's lids flashed open, focussing on an ominous shadow, slithering snake-like across the ceiling. He rubbed his eyes, slowly opening them in the hope that the shadow would be gone. Much to his dismay, the serpent's shade remained, coiled into a phantom-like spiral. His gaze widened, fixated on the serpent's hypnotic dance.

Shaking his head, he regained his senses and dived across his bedroom, flicking on the light switch. The room filled with light and the shadow disappeared. What was that thing? What could have caused it? Danny's imagination was working overtime. He ran over to the window and looking out of it, he noticed the street lamp outside of the house, its amber light licking at his window through a fine gap in the tree's branches.

"Could that be the cause of it?" Danny wondered out loud. He secretly hoped so.

However, he knew that there was only one way to find out for certain. He had to turn off the lights.

Slowly, he inched closer to the doorway; the sound of his rapid breathing filled the room. Procrastinating, his finger drew shapes around the light switch as he tried to find some deep, hidden bravery from within himself.

"Come on, Danny, you can do this," he said, giving himself a much needed pep talk.

He closed his eyes as sheer terror took control of his body's functions. His finger stopped on top of the switch and pushed it down with a click.

Through his eyelids, he could see that darkness had filled the room once again. His eyes slowly began to open for what he was sure would be the last time. The room was engulfed in gloom, somehow darker than before. Danny ran to the window and noticed that the street lamp had cut off, leaving the room in pitch blackness and luckily, without any shadows.

Tentatively crawling back into bed, Danny hoped for no more unpleasant surprises. He was still unsure of what he had just seen, or if he had seen anything at all, for that matter.

He lay down and rested his head, staring at the ceiling where the shadow had revealed itself just minutes earlier. There was no sign of anything unusual, yet still he laid there, his body full of adrenaline, aware of every sound around him.

As the night progressed, the weather outside worsened, the clouds thickened, dominating the sky with their dark presence. What began as a slight wind had grown into mighty gusts, rattling the old windows of Aunt Agnes' house and whistling through gaps in the roof tiles. The stubborn glow of the moon pushed through the clouds, casting light in rare intervals onto the trees and into the window of Danny's bedroom. A claw-like shadow was cast from the branches onto the wall above his bed, the deformed fingers almost reaching out for him in an attempt to pull him into their world of shade.

Finally sleeping peacefully, he was blissfully unaware of the exhibition of nature's force being displayed outside of his window.

Danny was awoken rudely that morning with droplets of water splashing onto his forehead from a leak in the roof. He rubbed his face on his blanket and rushed to find a container to put under the unwelcome droplets. He wasn't surprised to find a leak in his bedroom ceiling; he was actually more shocked that the house was still standing after being buffeted by the wind.

Walking downstairs, Danny knew he had to tell his Aunt Agnes about the leaky roof, before it caused any more damage. He would rather never speak to her again but he was worried that he would be sleeping under water if he didn't tell her soon.

"Aunt Agnes," he called out.

There was no response, much to his surprise.

"Aunt Agnes, there's a problem." Once again, he was met with silence.

As he made his way to the bottom of the stairs, he noticed that the living room was empty so he turned toward the kitchen. He stopped sharply outside of the basement door. The floor was warm and moist underneath his feet. He slowly looked down but couldn't see anything below his knees. A thick green mist was oozing out from under the basement door and had covered the bottom half of his legs. He began to panic, running aimlessly up and down the corridor, before his brain decided on a plan of action. He opened the basement door and made his way carefully halfway down the fog covered stairs. Though the smoke had begun to make his eyes sting, he could see his Aunt Agnes with what looked like an oil lamp in her hand.

"Aunt Agnes, what are you doing?" he called out, worried.

Aunt Agnes placed the lamp down and extinguished the green flame with a swift blow. She charged up the stairs, grabbed Danny by the shirt and dragged him out of the basement.

"You are never to step foot in that basement again, do you hear me boy?" she warned.

"Why not? What were you doing in there?" he demanded.

Aunt Agnes patted him on the head, a plastic grin etched across her face.

"Such an inquisitive boy, aren't we? Well, if you must know, I was fixing something," she shared, innocently.

"The lamp?" Danny pushed the matter further.

"Lamp? Oh, young boy, that is not a lamp. That is Friar's Lantern,"

She ruffled his hair in a false sense of affection, before trailing off toward the living room. Danny was stunned by her behaviour. She was almost pleasant, which was most certainly out of character. Who was Friar? Why did she have his lantern? he wondered. He was about to walk away when he remembered the leak in the roof.

"Oh, Aunt Agnes, I have something to tell you." He prepared himself to deliver the bad news.

"What is it this time, boy?" She quickly returned to her old self.

"There's a leak in the roof. Water is getting into my bedroom." He braced himself for a sharp reply.

"Do you expect me, an old lady, to climb onto the roof and fix it? You are young and fit, you do it," she demanded.

Danny didn't know the first thing about fixing roof tiles, but he didn't question his aunt because deep down, he knew that it would allow him to be outside for a while. Excitement swept over him as he anticipated the fresh air filling his lungs.

Wasting no time at all, he pulled on his shoes, opened the front door and stepped outside for the first time in weeks. Cold air pricked his dry skin, like a thousand tiny needles. Placing his hands on his stomach, he took a deep breath, opening up his airways to the crisp, cool air. A smile spread across his face, exaggerated by his bright red cheeks at each point. He had always taken the outdoors for granted, but never again. Looking around the garden, he noticed an old wooden ladder wrapped up within an unruly bush. He took in one last breath of fresh air before beginning his work on the roof.

Grabbing the steps, Danny attempted to pull them free from the thicket but it proved to be a harder task than he'd envisioned. Using the nearby head of a broken shovel, he hacked away at the vines until they finally released their stubborn grip. Though he was exhausted already, he was happy to continue working, if it meant that he could stay outside. Carefully gripping the splintered wood, he desperately tried to set the ladder gently against the wall. A torrent of small stones crumbled down from above him as it clattered against the side of the house. Relieved to discover that he hadn't broken anything, Danny proceeded to climb toward the roof. The wood was old and unstable, creaking more and more, the higher he climbed. Looking down, his whole body froze. It was a lot higher that he'd anticipated. Closing his eyes, he took a deep breath to calm himself. He looked up. Noticing he was only four rungs from the top, he braced himself for the final lap of the climb. He raised his foot, but as he lifted it toward the next step, the whole structure slipped from underneath him. Flailing wildly, he desperately tried to find something to hold on to, but before he could save himself, the timber base dug into the mud and stopped sliding. Terror evident on his face, he looked down once again to see Merelda sat below, her jade green eyes, looking back at him.

Luckily, he hadn't slid too far away, so Danny could still reach the roof from the top rung. Stretching, he carefully, pulled himself up, his hands struggling to grip onto the coat of slippery, green moss. Glancing at the shingles, he could see that one or two had slid out of place during the previous night's storm. Careful with every step, he eased his way closer toward the leak, his feet still slipping beneath him. He was amazed to discover there was only a single misplaced slate, even more amazing however was that he'd made it there in one piece. Though he was still unsure how to fix a roof, he tried the only thing he could. Placing a hand beneath the tile, he pushed hard against it, and to his surprise it slid right back into place. Feeling very pleased with himself, he inspected his work; however, his concentration was abruptly broken by a timid voice.

"Hey, you. What you doing all the way up there?"

Stunned, Danny turned too abruptly, lost his footing, and he slid downward, picking up speed at an alarming rate. Nearing the end, his feet made contact with the ladder, sending it crashing to the ground below. Danny clawed at the tiles, hoping to find something to hold onto, however, the moss just made his hands slimy and he slid helplessly off the edge.

FIVE

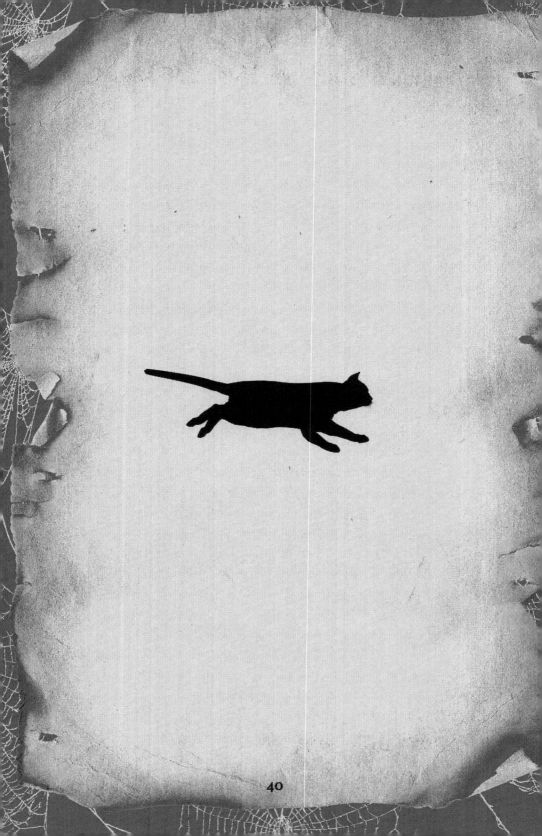

FIVE

Daring to breathe a sigh of relief, Danny looked up at his fingertips. Lit up a bright shade of purple, they held precariously to the gutter. A desperate squeak escaped from within him as he struggled to maintain his grip.

"Are you okay?" the same voice asked.

Danny couldn't believe his ears. Did he look okay? He was hanging helplessly from a roof.

"Oh, yes. I've never been better," he replied, sarcastically.

"Are you always this impolite?" the voice enquired, curiously.

"No, just when I'm hanging on to the edge of a building for dear life," Danny answered, somehow becoming even more sarcastic.

"Well, I have to say, it's not very smart being rude to the only person around to help you, now is it?"

Danny thought about that for a moment before stubbornly trying to pull himself up onto the roof in a futile attempt to prove that he didn't need anybody's help. After finally accepting that he would indeed need help, he looked down nervously to see who his rescuer would be. What stood below, surprised him; a delicate looking girl, about his age, with messy red hair, big glasses, and an army of freckles each fighting for position on her pale face.

The red headed girl picked up the ladder and placed it against the side of the house, sliding it gently between the wall and Danny, who was quick to kick off the top rung and push himself back up to safety. Slowly turning around, he sat down, his tired legs dangling aimlessly over the side.

"Thank you for helping me. I could have done it on my own though, eventually," Danny claimed, his pride as sore as his fingertips.

"Of course you could. You were just hanging there for fun, I'm sure," the red-headed girl replied, giving Danny a taste of his own medicine.

"Now who's being sarcastic?" Danny grinned.

"Not nice, is it?" the young girl scolded him.

"I'm sorry. I'm Danny by the way." He desperately tried to change the subject.

"I'm Pip. I live down the road. Do you live here now?" she asked cautiously, a look of concern etched on her face.

Danny considered the question for a while before realising that he didn't have an accurate answer to it.

"I-I don't know. I hope not," he stammered, a sadness pulling heavily at his chest. What if he did live here now? He didn't know where his family were, so maybe he was stuck here with his miserable Aunt Agnes. Danny quickly wiped a tear away from his eye before Pip could notice, after all, he didn't want her thinking he was a cry-baby.

"How can you not know where you live, Danny?" A look of confusion found its way onto her gentle face.

"Well, it's a long story but I suppose I have plenty of time to tell you." Danny took a deep breath, preparing himself to relive the horrors of Aunt Agnes, whilst Pip sat on the wall, patiently waiting to relive them with him.

"Well, it all started-"

"Where are you, boy?" a sharp shriek tore into Danny's concentration, instantly stopping his story. The colour faded from his cheeks as the shambling steps of Aunt Agnes drew closer.

"You have to get out of here. She won't be happy if she knows I'm talking to somebody." A wave of panic washed over Danny as he considered hiding on the roof.

"Who won't be happy, and why?" Pip jumped up from the wall and ran out of the garden.

"Aunt Agnes, she's coming. Go, now," Danny pleaded, desperately.

"I'll come back later." Pip grinned mischievously at Danny before running off, down the street.

"Where are you, pest?" Aunt Agnes was so close now; he could almost feel the venom in her words.

Danny climbed slowly and carefully down the ladder, his heart pounding in his chest. As he descended, he noticed he was panting heavily, whether it were out of exhaustion or fear, however, he did not know. Finally placing his feet on solid ground, he sighed, happy to be safe and sound, but sad that he would soon be back indoors for what could be another month. Kicking a small stone in protest, it rolled awkwardly, stopping as it hit a pair of fluffy, pink slippers. Danny recognised the slippers instantly; he knew that they were the only thing covering Aunt Agnes' crooked, witch-like toes.

"So, there you are pest. You've been hiding from me no doubt. I've had to do all of the chores inside the house myself. All the while, you're out here playing? This isn't a summer camp, boy. You either work for what I give you or I'll have you sleeping in the back yard."

Once again, Danny knew that he had been fixing the roof and almost fell off whilst trying. He also knew however, that answering back would only make things worse, so he-

"I have not been playing. I have been doing your dirty work out here. I've fixed the roof that was leaking on my head while I tried to sleep under old, dusty blankets, in the smallest, dirtiest room in the house. I almost fell off the roof and died until Pip saved me, not that you'll care." Danny couldn't believe what he was hearing. He had finally had enough and was standing up for himself. It felt good but deep down he knew it wouldn't end well.

"Pip, eh? A new friend is she?"

Staggered by his aunt's calm reply to his outburst, he didn't know what to say. "Y-yes," he squeaked, almost forgetting to stand his ground.

BANSHEE IN THE BASEMENT

Sensing weakness his aunt smiled wryly, her dry lips cracking as they slithered across her face. "Well then, it can be no coincidence that you've made a new friend and feel you are now big and brave enough to answer me back, boy. Therefore, you've left me with no choice in the matter. You will not see that young hooligan again, pest, is that clear?" Danny had set something inside Aunt Agnes' ablaze as she spat out her demands with malice.

"But-" Danny dared to reply but was cut off instantly.

"You will go up to your room where you will stay until I say otherwise. Now remove yourself from my presence, pest, I do not wish to be repeatedly reminded of how much skin was wasted on you."

Aunt Agnes' words burned every inch of Danny, as anger bubbled inside of his chest like he'd never felt before. He wanted to continue fighting the battle, but he feared what could have happened if he were to answer back again, so instead, he nodded in defeat and walked inside, his head bowed, staring at his feet.

He slammed the door to his room in one last act of defiance and threw himself down onto his bed. In an attempt to take out some of his rage, he

46

punched his paper-thin pillow and threw it across the room. Fury evident on his face, Danny lay staring at the damp patch on the ceiling, where the leaking water had dripped onto his head the night before. For once he wasn't thinking of his mother and how much he missed her, instead he was thinking of the endless list of horrible things Aunt Agnes had done and how miserable had she made him. The more he thought about her, the more his blood boiled and the more aggressive his breathing became. Though his body weighed heavy from a day of hard labour and fresh air, he struggled to find comfort. Eventually, however, he found relief from the tossing and turning, the panting levelling out as he slipped into a restless sleep.

A deafening clatter echoed across the room causing Danny to sit bolt upright, his vision still a blur. Half asleep and unsure of his whereabouts, he rubbed his eyes in a desperate attempt to regain his bearings, yet before he could gather his thoughts, another clatter filled the room.

SIX

"**M**erelda, what have you broken this time?" As always, Danny was quick to blame the cat.

Looking around his room, he was startled to discover that she was nowhere to be found. Panic rapidly setting in, he leapt out of bed and rushed to the window, staring out in perfect time to see a small rock tearing towards him. Falling to the floor, a look of horror struck his face as it clattered against the glass once again. Beginning to feel like a coward, he slowly peeled himself off the floor and tentatively looked out of the port hole in the window again. Much to his surprise, there stood Pip, with a hand full of small stones and a ball tucked firmly under her arm, a familiar mischievous grin setting her face aglow. She motioned with her free hand for him to come outside and greet her, but knowing that he had no way to escape his aunt's firm grasp, he shrugged back helplessly. Smiling compassionately, she signalled for him to open his window. Grabbing a nearby pen, Danny desperately looked for a sheet of paper to scribble a message upon. Thinking for a moment, Danny's eyes widened as a great idea filled his head. He reached over and ripped some of the old, peeling wallpaper from the wall, his tongue creeping out of his mouth as he began to write on it. Holding the newly penned sign up to the window, he mouthed the word 'locked' as though it would somehow confirm the written message.

Pip shrugged at Danny, brushing the stones out of her hand and onto the ground, the disappointment obvious in her face.

Lost within his thoughts, Danny took a step back from the window and sat on the bottom of his bed. Before he could get comfortable however, he sprung back up to his feet and ran across the hall into the bathroom, locking the door behind him.

"Don't be in that bathroom all night, boy. There may be three in this house, but they all belong to me." Aunt Agnes' spite seemed to get worse every day. Luckily, he seemed to get better at ignoring her.

Once again taking no notice of his shrieking aunt, Danny stepped onto the toilet and attempted to open the window. He was disappointed but not at all surprised to discover that it was locked. Refusing to give up, however, he turned his attention to the window ledge where he noticed three green vases of varying sizes, filled with dying flowers.

"The key must be around here somewhere," Danny whispered to himself.

Rolling up his sleeve, he slowly lowered his hand past the wilted tulips and into the murky, old water of the first vase, grimacing as the cold numbed his fingers. Feeling around aimlessly, Danny suddenly felt something drop from the browning leaves and onto his arm. Assuming it was a droplet of water, he didn't panic, instinctively attempting to brush it off instead. The panic did come however when it crawled onto his hand. Looking down, instead of water, he was greeted by the glaring eyes of a huge, hairy spider, piercing into his deepest fears. Trying desperately not to scream or shout, Danny shook his hand frantically, causing the creature to drop onto the floor and scurry behind an old, rusted water pipe. A shiver ran through his entire being, every hair standing to attention. He hated all creepy crawlies, but spiders were the worst, and he knew that he still had two more vases to look inside if he wanted to find the key and escape.

Finally gaining some control over his breathing, Danny tried to muster some extra bravery from deep inside of him, though every time he went to reach inside the second vase, he'd picture the spider staring at him and itch all over.

Out of nowhere an idea washed over Danny like a bucket of ice cold water. Why didn't he think of it, earlier?

"Please, be under here. Please, be under here," Danny pleaded with his own fate.

Reaching over to the first vase, he tipped it slightly, but much to his disappointment only a dead leaf rested on the underside. Looking over at the third, it was much too small to house a key underneath it, meaning the second was his only hope. Fully aware that his number of options was rapidly running out, Danny's heart began to pound. Slowly reaching over to the vase, he placed his hand around its neck and tipped it gently to the side. Danny couldn't believe his luck. Underneath, in a small puddle, lay a piece of rusted metal, rugged around the edges. Allowing himself a subtle smile, Danny grabbed the key and cupped it in his hands as though it were the rarest of gems.

Looking up, he noticed that just as the window in his bedroom, there was a small key hole in the centre of the handle. Much like the key, it was badly rusted, which posed the obvious question, will it still work? Danny knew there was only one way to be sure but he almost didn't want to try. A deep breath later, though, he persuaded the key into the old lock with some extra force. To his surprise, the key turned first time and the lock released. Not wasting a second, Danny twisted the handle and gave the stiff, old window an almighty push. Creaking in protest, it opened an inch or two but refused to budge any further. Frustration swept over him and he forcefully pushed the window with all of his strength and anger. With a final groan, the hinges buckled and jammed his only exit in place. Danny was devastated.

"Is that you, Danny?" Pip's familiar, timid voice crept in through the tiny gap in the window.

Peering out with one eye, he could see her sitting on the wall with a pink ball under her arm. "Yes, it's me. I'm trying to find a way out of here. I found the key to this window even though it was protected by a giant spider that tried to eat me." He cringed at the thought.

"Let me guess, it's stuck. Oh, and spiders don't eat people," Pip giggled.

"Aren't you going to say anything helpful?" Danny snapped, irritably.

"Of course, I am. Don't you know that old windows are all the same? If the key works in that window, it will most likely work in your bedroom, too." Proud of herself, Pip grinned.

"I knew that," Danny reassured her, his pride bruised once again.

Grabbing the key from the window and dropping it into his pocket, he jumped down and ran for the door, his eyes never leaving the spider for fear he would be eaten. Dashing through to his bedroom, he quickly closed the door behind him.

Wasting no time, he charged over to the window, grabbed the key from his pocket, and jammed it into the lock. But this time, it wouldn't turn. Taking a deep breath he desperately tried to steady his shaking hands, it already seemed like it had been a long day and his body just wasn't used to being active any more. Trying again, the key twisted smoothly in the lock and the handle sprung open. Breathing a sigh of relief, Danny placed both hands on the window, his sweaty palms creating prints on the glass.

"Come on, please work this time," Danny mumbled to himself.

Pushing at the window, he could barely move it. Wiping his perspiration onto his trousers, he once again placed his hands upon the cobweb coated window. Determined not to fail, he let out a mighty grunt, pushing with every drop of energy he had left. With an almighty crack, the window swung open and clattered against the outer wall. Danny was so happy that he almost felt like dancing. He knew that he still had to find a way to remove the metal bars, however as they stood firmly to attention like a row of soldiers blocking his path. He was thin enough to fit through, if only he could remove one of them. Grabbing the bars, he began frantically shaking them one by one, hoping that he would somehow be strong enough to rip one of them off. Reaching the last, exhaustion was setting in as he could barely find the strength to lift his arms.

"Come on, Danny. It's either you find the energy, or you stay here in Aunt Agnes' home made prison." That was all that he needed to persuade him to try one last time; reaching out to the only bar he was yet to try, he gripped it firmly with both hands and shook it desperately. Danny gasped; he could hear a faint rattling coming from both ends of the bar. Looking it up and down, he noticed that the screws in the top and bottom loosened with every shake. Deep down, he knew that if he were to keep shaking it, the noise would alert his Aunt Agnes who would then come tearing up the stairs to intervene. Instead, he decided it would be best to look around for a tool to remove the screws. After trying a series of unusual objects, Danny's eyes locked on the key in the window. Grabbing it, quickly he placed it in the head of the screw. Whilst it was far from perfect, if he was gentle, it might just work. With careful yet determined twists the screws began to loosen more and more before eventually falling to the floor, one by one. Danny pulled at the bar one last time and the stubborn soldier finally stood down, leaving a gap just big enough for him to squeeze through.

A hollow feeling in his core told him that it wouldn't be long until Aunt Agnes was banging on the door and yelling at him about the bathroom window being open. He had to find a way down and fast.

"Pip, Pip, it worked," he shouted, excitedly.

"That's great. Now what do we do?" she asked, hoping that he had a plan.

"Grab the ladder and put it against the window, quick," he barked, stopping abruptly in his tracks as he heard an unfamiliar noise in the hall. Holding his breath, he listened carefully. As the noise repeated, he was relieved to discover that it was just Merelda, scratching and clawing at his door. He dared to breathe again.

"The ladder is ready, I think." Pip didn't sound too confident.

The wooden ladder was much too tall, reaching up past his bedroom, so she had placed it at an unusual angle with the feet buried in the mud. Squeezing through the gap in the bars, Danny sat precariously on the window ledge whilst trying to find his footing on the ladder. Just as he was beginning to feel confident that he wouldn't fall, his bedroom door swung open and his Aunt Agnes glared at him from the doorway, eyes wide, lips curled into a snarl.

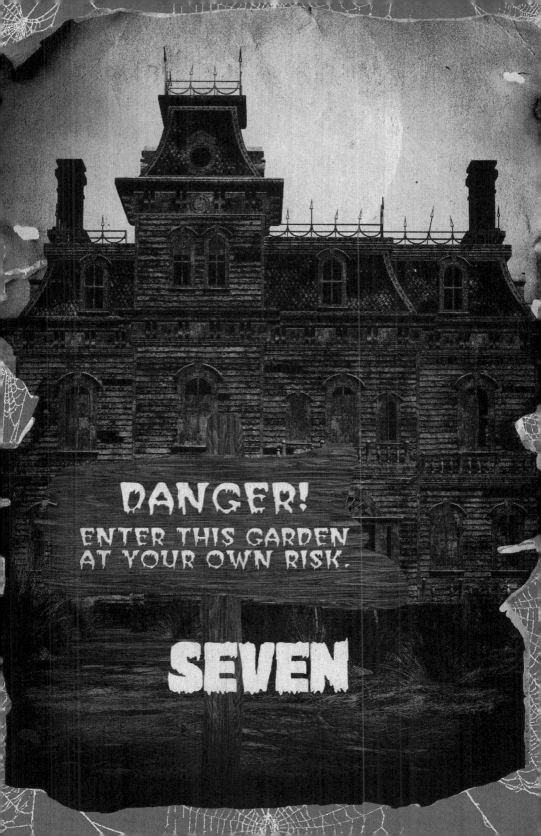

DANGER!
ENTER THIS GARDEN
AT YOUR OWN RISK.

SEVEN

SEVEN

"**W**hat do you think you're doing, boy? Get back in here, this instant," Aunt Agnes howled.

Stunned by the sudden appearance of his aunt, Danny lost his footing and slid on his bottom, down the ladder, and into the mud.

"Quick, let's go," Pip shouted, grabbing Danny by the wrist and dragging him down the street, away from Aunt Agnes' preying eyes.

Hiding behind a prickly bush a few houses away from Aunt Agnes, Danny and Pip panted, the fear of being chased causing their breath to escape them.

"Well, I'm out of that awful house, but what do we do now?" Danny asked between breaths.

"I could show you the town; after all you've only seen one street," Pip suggested, the concept of being his tour guide sounding fun to her.

"One house actually," he was quick to correct her.

Pip laughed, throwing her ball at Danny and hitting him right between the eyes. She giggled, playfully as he fell to the ground. Picking himself up, he kicked the ball as hard as he could at Pip but she ducked out of the way sending it soaring through the air before hitting a wooden sign and coming to rest in an unkempt flowerbed in the old man's garden.

"Oh, no. Not that house," Danny said, lines of worry crawling across his forehead.

"What's wrong with that house?" Pip asked innocently.

"The old man is up to something strange. I saw him arguing with somebody in that window, but then, well, and then they just disappeared." His words sounded ridiculous, even to him, but he knew he was telling the truth.

"Really? That's so cool. We have to investigate."

"What? No way. Just get your ball so we can get out of here," he argued, desperately.

"I'll be the detective and saying as you like spying on people, you can be my assistant," she declared, not taking no for an answer.

Before Danny could plead his case further, Pip had already skipped off toward the old man's garden. Sighing, Danny shuffled after her, dragging his feet in protest. As they neared, he looked around anxiously, the pit of his stomach quivering at the thought of being caught. Pip edged into the yard as Danny stared at the wooden sign, reading it aloud. "Danger! Enter this garden at your own risk."

"Shush. Do you want to get caught?" Pip whispered loudly.

She had collected her ball and was now heading towards the window at the front of the house. The room was dark, lit up only by a small television, a distorted voice bellowing out from beneath a screen filled with static. Taking a step back she noticed a flickering light silhouetting a cat in the upstairs windows, directly above.

"Let's sneak in and see what clues we can find," she said eagerly, jumping from one foot to the other.

"I'd really rather not. What if we get caught?" Danny replied, his sense of adventure drained away by a month of living with his aunt.

"We won't get caught, besides surely anything is better than going back to that house." Pip knew she was right, and Danny did too. Taking another deep breath, he plodded along behind her. Walking up to the front door, Pip gave it a determined push but it refused to budge.

"Ha! You're as weak as a kitten," Danny mocked.

"Well, Mister Strongman, why don't you give it a try?" she retorted.

"Fine, I will," mumbling under his breath, Danny spat on his hands for extra grip.

"That's disgusting," Pip chirped in from behind him.

Ignoring her, he placed both hands firmly on the door and with a loud grunt, began pushing as hard as he could.

"You should probably stop now. Your face has changed colour more times than a chameleon," Pip laughed.

Danny's arms fell to his sides in defeat as he finally remembered to breathe again, the deep shade of purple draining from his face.

"You looked like a giant grape. Oh, and now who's as weak as a kitten?" Pip laughed hysterically, pointing at his face.

"Why don't you just shut- wait a minute. Kitten? That's it!" Danny's face, now back to its normal shade, stretched into a triumphant smile.

"What are you talking about now?" Pip was beginning to find herself, confused more often than not with Danny around.

"The cat that we saw, sitting in the window upstairs. Where there's a cat, there must be a cat flap. Let's try the back door." Forgetting his fear, Danny ran around the outside of the house with Pip in tow, jumping over a small fence and heading into the back yard.

"See? I told you," Danny said, pointing at the cat flap, built into the back door.

"Alright, smarty pants, but is it open?" A small part of Pip hoped it wouldn't be, so she could mock Danny some more, but deep down she knew it was their only chance of getting into the house.

Using his foot, Danny nudged the flap, which in turn waved back and forth like a flag in the wind.

"It's open." Danny was pleased with himself. A little too pleased with himself actually, as he didn't think before starting to squeeze through the hole and into the house. As was almost expected, half way through the cat flap Danny stopped.

"Why have you stopped, is somebody there?" Pip asked nervously.

"No. Nobody is here," Danny replied quietly.

"Then, why on earth have you stopped?" Pip was getting impatient.

"I-I'm stuck. Give me a push with your foot." Danny's voice caught in his throat with embarrassment.

"No way. Your bottom is muddy and I don't want to get my shoes dirty," Pip giggled.

"Just kick me." Danny couldn't believe what he was saying.

Finally dislodged from the cat flap, Danny stood rubbing his sore bottom. Looking around he realised he was in the old man's kitchen. Sliding through the small entrance with ease, Pip walked toward Danny, her feet sticking to the black and white tiles on the floor. Standing beside him, they took a moment to survey their surroundings. Even through the darkness it was obvious that the kitchen hadn't been cleaned in a long while. Grease coated every surface and the smell was magnified by the constant buzzing of flies above their heads.

"I can't see a thing. Put the light on, would you?" Pip requested.

Looking up at the lighting fixture, Danny noticed a broken bulb hanging from the ceiling by worn out wires.

"I don't think it's such a good idea." Instead, he opened the refrigerator. Like an old torch, it shed its dull light across the centre of the kitchen, revealing mouldy food and dirty plates strewn from the sink across the countertop to a microwave that took centre stage, its door wide open, burnt food caked to the inside.

"This place is disgusting, let's get out of here," Danny suggested, his nose twitching at the smell.

"Well, we can't do that, can we? What kind of detectives would we be if we left without any clues?" Pip asked, light-heartedly.

Danny didn't know how she could treat this like some sort of game. Didn't she know there could be real danger in the house? Had she even seen how terrifying the old man was? Either way, he knew that he couldn't just leave her there, alone, so he continued to follow her.

Stepping into the front room, a cloud of dust flew up from the carpet engulfing their feet with every step they took, each speck with its own role in a unique formation. Trying not to cough, they each placed their sleeved arms over their faces. As they crept deeper inside, they began to notice a subtle beeping from near the window. They glanced toward one another, each confirming that they heard it too. Inching nervously closer, the noise became clearer and clearer with every reluctant step they took. Holding out his hand, Danny slowly reached toward a dusty, metal cabinet. He had noticed that with Pip around, he was almost back to his old brave self. Pulling the handle, it screeched open, the metal against metal like nails on a chalkboard. Slowly, he placed his hand inside and-

"What are you doing here?" the raspy yell, sent a shiver so strong down Danny's spine that he jumped backwards, his legs refusing to hold his weight, he crumpled to the floor. Pip snatched his hand and dragged him behind an old sofa.

"That's it, we're dead. The old man is going to find us," Danny said, giving up all hope of an escape.

Placing a finger to her lips, Pip shushed him and carefully crawled to the end of the sofa. Peering out from their hiding place, she was surprised to find that nobody was there.

"I said, what are you doing here?" the voice repeated itself.

Danny and Pip glared at each other, frozen with fear.

"What are we going to do?" Danny asked, unable to keep his voice steady.

"We have to get out of here, now," Pip decided.

Nodding toward the doorway, Pip signalled for Danny to lead the way. On his hands and knees, he began to crawl toward the door.

"How can you be so sure?" the voice bellowed, echoing down the old staircase.

"We have to trust him, we have no other choice," a second voice chimed in.

Upon hearing the second voice, Danny and Pip jumped up to their feet and scrambled out of the front door, their legs still shaking beneath them.

"When the time comes, he'll know what to do," the second voice continued.

Standing in the front yard, Danny looked up at the window to once again see two silhouettes yelling at each other.

"That's the same two people I saw before. Only last time he-"

Before Danny could finish, the second silhouette disappeared before their eyes, leaving nothing but a cloud of dust in his place.

"Disappeared," stunned, Pip finished his sentence for him.

EIGHT

EIGHT

Obliviously, they found themselves staggering backwards away from the old man's house, fuelled only by their desperation to escape. Exhausted, they tripped over one another and crashed to the ground in a crumpled heap.

"Are you alright?" Pip was first to ask.

"I'm fine, now. I can't believe we got away," Danny replied positively.

All positivity instantly drained from them as they were stopped by a harsh tugging at the backs of their shirts. Slowly looking up they were met with the menacing grin of Aunt Agnes, a web of facial hair clinging to her lip. She had found them.

Staring into the unforgiving, black eyes of his aunt, Danny wondered with dread, what her next move could possibly be. He didn't have to wonder for long however, as she began dragging them by the shirts toward her house.

"What are you doing? Let me go," Pip demanded.

"Be quiet, hooligan. You two are coming with me," Aunt Agnes declared, dragging them away like a giant spider would its prey.

"I'm not going with you. You can't drag me like this," Pip protested.

"You should be punished for your actions, hooligan, and if I must be the one to deliver it, then so be it," Aunt Agnes threatened her new victim.

Kicking open the front door, Aunt Agnes dragged Danny and Pip into her home-made prison and slammed the door closed.

"Go to your room, pest. I believe me and your new friend should have a little heart to heart."

"You have no heart and I won't leave her with you," Danny said, defiantly.

"Don't make it worse, Danny. Just do as she says, I think she's crazy," Pip said, attempting to paint a reassuring smile upon her face.

"Do as the girl says, boy. Go to your room, now. I'll deal with you later," Aunt Agnes warned.

Pip nodded at Danny, who in turn nodded back before slowly backing up the stairs and into his room.

Stood with his ear pressed firmly against the door, Danny desperately tried to listen in on what was happening downstairs, but all he could hear was the pounding of his own heartbeat. Giving up, he backed away from the door and sat on the corner of his bed, confusion evident on his face. What had happened at the old man's house? More importantly, was Pip, alright? He desperately wanted to charge downstairs and make sure, but he knew that he'd only make matters worse.

Danny's entire bedroom shook as a thunderous bang rumbled around the house. Shocked, Danny leapt up to his feet, ripped open his door, and tore downstairs as fast as his exhausted legs would carry him.

"Pip? Aunt Agnes? What was that noise?" Danny asked, charging into the living room to find his Aunt Agnes sat, as always, in her favourite chair with her legs outstretched, pink slippers resting upon a footstool.

Danny's mind was working overtime yet he still didn't seem to understand anything. What was that noise? Was there even a noise at all? Was he hearing things? He had to find out for sure even if it meant talking to Aunt Agnes.

"A-Aunt Agnes?" Danny stuttered.

"I was wondering when you'd show up for your turn, pest," Aunt Agnes spat.

"What was that bang? Where's Pip?" He had a

thousand more questions he wanted to ask but knew he must prioritise and only ask a few.

"What am I, your secretary? I'm not here to answer your questions, pest. Now sit down and let's have a little talk," she demanded, pointing a crooked finger at a wooden stool in the corner.

"Not until you tell me where Pip is." Danny was in no rush to sit down, he was well aware that Aunt Agnes' idea of a talk was nothing pleasant.

"She went home. Now, sit," she barked, her patience rapidly deteriorating.

"I don't believe you. What did you do to her?" Danny was surprised to notice he was yelling at her.

"You disobedient little oaf. Sit down!"

Noticing the fire in her glare, Danny promptly sat down and awaited his scolding. Aunt Agnes shuffled back in her chair and took a sip of the steaming, green drink she loved so much.

"Now then, boy. First things first, you will not run off like that again, are we clear?"

"Maybe if-"

"Are we clear?" Aunt Agnes was obviously in no mood for arguments.

"Yes, Aunt Agnes," Danny said, not entirely sure he meant it.

"Good. Secondly, as a much deserved apology to me, you will do extra chores. From now on, you will clean up the front yard of litter and rake any leaves into a neat pile out of the way."

"Oh, fine. I won't be here much longer anyway." Danny regretted the words as soon as they passed his lips.

"Oh yes, that reminds me," Aunt Agnes pushed her footstool away and leaned forward in her chair, a yellowing tongue slithered passed her gums and slowly moistened her cracked lips before she continued, "I've just talked to your mother-" she began before Danny jumped in excitedly.

"What did she say? Is she alright?" Danny felt a weight lift from his shoulders.

"Well, I'm old and my memory is not what it used to be but let's see now. She thanked me for taking such good care of you and asked if I wouldn't mind continuing to do so as she won't be back from a long, long time."

Danny was crushed, the weight on his shoulders suddenly doubled.

"W-Why?"

"What does it matter? The bottom line is, you're stuck with your dear old Aunt Agnes for the foreseeable future, boy. You belong to me. Now, go to bed."

Danny couldn't believe it. Why would his mother leave him with this woman? Surely, she must have known how horrible she would be to him. Feeling exhausted and defeated, he dragged himself upstairs, barely able to lift his feet from one step to the next. Shuffling into his room, he swung his door closed and climbed onto his bed. Curling up into a ball in an attempt to avoid all of the old springs in his mattress, exhaustion finally took over his body and darkness engulfed him as he fell into an unhappy sleep. Even whilst asleep it was as though he could feel how unhappy he was, his memories creeping into his dreams, the world weighing heavy upon his chest. He knew he couldn't give up and let his aunt win; he had to do something.

A huge crash shook his room once again, waking Danny with such a fright that he fell out of bed and onto the floor. Staggering up to his feet, he knew that he should check downstairs but his body filled with an irrational urge to look out of his window. Finding the port hole he'd made earlier, he looked out to see the old man standing in the garden across the street, frantically waving his arms and repeatedly mouthing the word 'No.'

Why was the old man warning him? What if it's a trick? Knowing he couldn't trust him, Danny chose to ignore him instead, creeping silently out of his room and to the top of the staircase. Peering over the banister, he looked downstairs. In the darkness, he noticed a figure reaching out toward the basement door. Danny gasped, instantly holding both hands up to his mouth. Seeming not to have heard him, the figure grabbed the basement key and turned it, locking the door.

"It must be Aunt Agnes. I better go back to bed before she sees me," Danny whispered, his own voice reassuring him.

Rubbing his eyes, he turned to walk away but as he did, the figure vanished, turning to dust and disappearing under the basement door.

NINE

Sitting up in bed, his blanket wrapped tightly around him for security, Danny knew he wouldn't be unable to sleep tonight. His mind filled with images so confusing he couldn't be sure how real they actually were. One emotion, however, dominated even his confusion; fear. Whilst he was understandably terrified, he wasn't scared for his own safety, he feared for the wellbeing of his friend Pip. Aunt Agnes had assured him that Pip had run home, but her history of compulsive lying had given him no reason to trust her word. As far as he was concerned, Pip could be anywhere. What if Aunt Agnes had done something horrible to her? One thing he knew for sure, and the only clear thought in an otherwise chaotic mind was, he had to escape again and find her, but how? He knew Aunt Agnes would be awake and wreaking havoc on him by seven in the morning, so he needed to escape before then. Looking over the edge of his bed he saw his clock lying on the floor; a blanket of shattered plastic surrounded it.

"It must have smashed when that loud noise shook the room. I knew I wasn't imagining it," Danny said, relieved to know that he wasn't going crazy.

Confirmation that the explosive noises had

actually happened was a huge relief to him and gave the confidence boost he would need to find Pip and discover the truth behind the old man across the street.

The morning light began shedding its warmth into Danny's room, declaring that it was time to leave. Climbing out of bed, he threw on his coat and shoes, his hand getting stuck in the sleeve as he rushed out of his bedroom door and down the stairs. Freeing himself from the clothing, he unlocked the front door and opened it as quietly and silently as his shaking hands would allow. He slid through the slight gap and pulled it gently closed with a click that rattled like a gunshot as it tore through the morning silence.

Hoping desperately that he hadn't awoken his aunt, Danny walked out of the front yard just far enough to be out of the view of her windows. As he began his trek down the street, it dawned on him.

"I can't believe it. I don't even know where Pip lives. I know she lives down the street somewhere, but I don't know where," Danny sighed. If only he had taken the time to ask her, but he just wasn't used to talking to people his own age. Making friends had never come easy to him, he didn't know what to say to people, and therefore, he'd always been cast aside. Pip was different though;

she was easy to talk to and had never judged him when he said something silly. He had to find her.

His thoughts were abruptly interrupted by the sound of shuffling footsteps. As Danny looked up he noticed a frail, elderly man walking down the footpath away from his house, his gown waving in the morning breeze, slippers dragging across the concrete slabs. Stopping, the old man tightened the belt of his robe before looking up at Danny with clouded eyes.

"Good morning, son," the elderly man greeted Danny politely.

"Good morning, sir. I wonder if I could bother you for a moment," Danny enquired.

"If you could make it quick, that would be grand. It's a bit cold to be standing around chatting in my pyjamas." One side of his face twitched into a crooked smile.

"Of course, sir. I was just wondering if you knew of a young girl that lives around here called Pip. She's my best friend and I don't know where she is." Worry crept into Danny's voice.

"I dare say that she's not the best of friends if you don't even know where she lives." The elderly man's statement was conclusive. Danny nodded, looking around in the hope that he'd see Pip in one of the many windows in the street.

"Thank you for your time." Danny couldn't believe his eyes as he turned. The elderly man was gone. There had been no goodbye and no shuffling from his feet. In his place, lay a mound of dust and dirt, shrinking smaller with every whisper from the morning wind.

Backing away, Danny's face turned a sickly shade as the colour drained from it.

"What is going on, around here?" Danny asked himself, determined to get to the bottom of it. "Whatever it is, I'm sure that Pip and the old man is the key to finding out," he decided.

Stopping to think for a moment, he finally gathered a plan of action within his mind. It was surprisingly simple, really. He didn't know where Pip was, or where she lived, meaning that he had no sensible place to start looking for her. However, he suspected that the old man must be behind all of this, and starting at his house could lead to finding Pip.

Pushing back his fear, Danny crept slowly across the road, toward the old man's house, the wooden sign still taking pride of place in the centre of his lawn. Reaching the yard, he took a deep breath, steadying himself before stepping gently onto the grass. Looking through the front window, he was surprised to learn that nothing at all had changed. A thick layer of dust still coated the carpet and the television still lit up the room as it showed only static.

"Well, this isn't helping at all. I have to go inside, again," Danny whispered, almost trying to convince himself that it was a good idea.

Looking around to make sure nobody was watching, he jumped over the small fence to the side of the house and slunk around to the back. Lowering himself down to all fours, he prepared to enter the house through the cat flap once more. He sighed, steadying himself and held his breath as he crawled toward the door. Falling backwards with a thud, he rubbed the top of his head. The cat flap was locked. Now what was he going to do? He had no other way of getting into the house. Looking around, he scanned for open doors or windows but to no avail. His only option was to look through the glass and hope that he could find an answer to his many questions.

Staring into the kitchen, he once again noticed that nothing had changed. The microwave still stood centre stage with its door wide open and ancient food burned to the inside. The old man must live upstairs and never come down, but how does he eat without the use of a kitchen?

"You must leave, now," a raspy voice, bellowed from within the walls of the house. Noticing there was no escape from the backyard, Danny jumped back and ran around the front of the house.

"Leave, now, before he sees you," the voice warned.

Every thread of Danny's being wanted to run away, but he would never have the answers he needed if he did. He had to continue what he started. Marching toward the house, he saw a mailbox built into the door. Determination taking control of him, he squatted down, opened the mail flap, and stared into the house.

"Now!" the voice screamed.

A cloud of dust exploded through the mailbox and blanketed Danny's face. Falling backwards he began hacking uncontrollably and rolling around on the ground, a sharp pain tearing through his chest. His eyes were open, but he couldn't see, he tried to get air through his mouth but no amount of oxygen seemed enough. Desperately, he crawled away from the house, his head spinning, chest tight from coughing. Reaching out for help, his hand rested on a small, olive green shrub at the edge of the garden. Instinct took over as he frantically rubbed his face on the soft foliage, in a final attempt to regain his senses. The choking continued as he crumpled to the ground, panic setting in.

"Can't you read the sign?" the similar raspy voice yelled as the old man threw a bucket of ice cold water from an upstairs window, soaking Danny from head to toe. The shock from the freezing water caused every muscle in his body to tense up. As he lay curled up in a ball, aching but no longer coughing, he looked up to see the old man slam the window closed and become hidden behind a sheet of dirt on the glass.

TEN

TEN

Though he knew the task was not complete, he was much too sore to continue. Chest tightening with every breath and muscles aching more with every step, he struggled back to his Aunt Agnes' house, hoping desperately that she had not awoken, yet.

One arm resting on his aching ribs offered some support as he attempted to take some much needed deep breaths. Using his other arm, he gently nudged open the front door, slithering in through the tiny gap he had allowed himself. Begging for silence, he carefully eased the door closed, and slowly turned to make his way back up to his room before his aunt could discover he was gone. As he turned, however, he was stunned to find Aunt Agnes exiting the basement and abruptly locking the door behind her.

"Almost done, and then the lantern can finally be opened." The look of self-glorification on her face, made Danny feel sick.

"What is almost done?" he asked.

Aunt Agnes gasped, shocked by his presence. He took a small amount of pleasure in frightening her for a change but tried not to grin about it too much.

"If anybody should be asking the questions here, it's me. Where have you been hiding all day, boy? Why are you covered in dirt?" Aunt Agnes probed expertly.

"I-I was tidying up the garden, just like you told me to. I woke up early this morning and thought I'd give you a nice surprise to wake up to." Danny hoped that she would, miraculously, believe his tale.

"You can't butter me up that easily, pest. Now, kindly get out of my sight, I've had a good day and I don't want you ruining it." She looked him up and down and with a single snort, shambled toward her favourite chair.

"A good day? But it's only morning." Confused, Danny charged into the front room and stared at the old, wooden clock on the wall, the hands obviously deceiving him.

"Five o'clock. How is that possible? How could I have missed a whole day?" Admittedly, on the way back to his aunt's house, he had been much too sore to notice the sun going down, but to miss a whole day? That's a different matter entirely. Just as he thought his mind was filled with unanswered questions, more began to swim around in there. However, no unsolved puzzle was more important to him than the whereabouts of his friend Pip. Whilst he wanted to tear out of the door and begin searching for her again, he was made aware through his aching muscles that he was too exhausted to be of any use to her tonight.

Making his way tentatively upstairs, his legs becoming heavier with every step, he stumbled into the bathroom almost slipping on the damp floor. His entire body exhausted, he perched on the edge of the bathtub. Eyes weighing heavy, he grabbed a nearby washcloth with a shaking hand and began the arduous process of removing every dust particle from his face and clothes. Feeling refreshed but still every bit as sore, he struggled from the bathroom and wobbled through his bedroom door, falling face down onto his bed. His intention was to create a fool proof plan to assist in finding Pip the following day, however weariness had finally defeated him and he was asleep before he could even contemplate it.

What felt like minutes but may have been hours passed before he was forcefully jerked awake. Stunned but alert, he could sense that something wasn't right; his own muscles had violently shaken him awake. Though it felt like such a challenging task, he forced his heavy eyes open. Despite his muscles aching and his blurred vision, he could still make out the sharp moonlight as it forced itself in through the window, glistening against the coat of sweat blanketing his face.

Sitting up, Danny felt awful. His throat was dry, his head pounded, and he felt as though he had very little control over his limbs as his muscles tensed, contracting of their own accord.

Fighting through the discomfort Danny forced himself to his feet and, placing a shaking hand against the wall, searched for his balance. As he straightened up, a thick stream of dust poured down from his shoulders and landed gently upon the carpet. Where had that come from? He was sure that he had removed all of the dust from his face and clothing the previous night before collapsing into his bed. Shaking his head, he staggered out of the room, too sick to ask questions. Reaching the top of the staircase he teetered dangerously close to the edge of the steps. Quickly, he gripped onto the banister with both hands, clumsily but safely easing his exhausted body down the stairs one by one. Eventually reaching the bottom, he sighed with relief before shuffling delicately toward the kitchen, inching closer to a much needed cool drink. His mouth was so dry now that his tongue stuck to the roof of his mouth. Feeling the cold tiles of the kitchen floor beneath his bare feet sent shivers throughout his already twitching body. Filling a nearby glass from the faucet, he frantically gulped down every drop, without stopping to breathe.

With his thirst quenched, the torturous

symptoms began to ease. The muscle spasms calmed to an occasional twitch, leaving Danny's legs heavy but functional, allowing him to walk with less discomfort back toward the staircase. Exiting the kitchen, he trudged past the basement door where he was suddenly alerted by the faint but distinctive sound of knocking. Stopping mid-step, he held his foot aloft so as not to interrupt his concentration with any other noise. Pushing his ear against the basement door, he found himself still unable to focus due to the unforgiving throbbing travelling throughout his skull.

"Get away from there, boy. There's nothing in that basement for you," Aunt Agnes screeched from the top of the stairs, her shrill voice piercing every aching fibre of his being.

"I wasn't going in the basement; I was feeling unwell and came to get a glass of water," Danny lied, his hoarse voice scratching at his dry throat as he spoke.

"A likely story, pest." The words oozed from her crooked mouth, like poison from a wound as she shuffled ever closer. Stopping suddenly, her eyes narrowed replacing her usual chilling glare with a look of judgement and disgust as she examined him up and down.

"The fever is upon you, boy," she said, her

eyes narrowing further.

"The fever, what fever?" he searched for answers.

"It's just a matter of time," Aunt Agnes declared with pleasure, stepping between Danny and the basement door. Extending a crooked finger she pointed up the stairs ordering him abruptly back to bed. Danny, too exhausted to argue, did as his aunt demanded and headed for his bedroom.

"Oh yes, just a matter of time," she repeated as a vile grin stretched across her face.

ELEVEN

ELEVEN

The following morning, Danny woke feeling refreshed, noticing as soon as his eyes opened that he felt remarkably healthy; no headaches, no aching muscles and despite what his aunt had said; no fever. Sitting up, he carefully swung his legs over the side of the bed and allowed himself a gentle stretch, worried that any sudden movements would trigger his muscles to ache again. It would seem, though, that he had somehow gotten over all of his symptoms overnight. All, except for one that is; his right hand was a little numb. Blinking his vision clear, he held both hands out in front for a quick assessment. Staring from left to right multiple times, he couldn't believe what he was seeing, his eyes widening as the reality of his predicament set in.

"My hand, what happened to it? It's transparent. I can see right through it!" Danny yelled, hysterical. Was this the fever, his aunt had warned him of? He was almost certain that she had just been trying to scare him.

Charging downstairs, Danny barged into the front room to confront Aunt Agnes, as she sat, as always, in her favourite chair.

"Aunt Agnes. What has happened to my hand?" Danny asked desperately.

"How am I supposed to know, pest? What do you think I am, a mind reader?" Aunt Agnes mocked him, mercilessly.

"Look at my hand. You were talking about me having the fever last night and now this happens. That is just a bit too coincidental, don't you think?" Determined to get the answers he required, he wasn't going to let her evade him this time, so he held his transparent hand up to her face.

"Oh, well would you look at that. Isn't that strange?" She continued to thrive upon his suffering.

"I know that you know something about this. Please, tell me what's happening!"

"Well, it's very simple, boy, they have found you," she teased, offering a snippet of the information he needed.

"Who, who have found me?" he pleaded.

"It's just a matter of time. A matter of time until you join them, boy, until you become one of them." Aunt Agnes glared right through Danny, a wretched smile forming on her thin, cracked lips.

"What can we do? You have to stop this," Danny begged.

"We? It's nothing to do with me, boy. This is your problem, you deal with it." She leaned back in her chair, closing her eyes as she shuffled around in search for comfort.

Terrified, Danny backed out of the room and headed for the kitchen. Suddenly he was thirsty again. Noticing the glass he had drank from the previous night, he reached out to pick it up, only for it to pass right through his transparent right hand. Still unable to believe his eyes, Danny repeatedly swiped his hand through the glass. Beginning to feel light headed, he pulled out a chair and slumped down into it.

"I have to come up with a plan, I can't just give up. What if I turn completely transparent? What if I disappear? I have to fix this." Danny was petrified but his mother called him stubborn with good reason; he would not give up. Sat with his head in his single remaining hand, he started to think about all of the unfortunate occurrences that had affected him recently. The fever had come to him from the old man's house, but he knew that there was no way in.

"The basement, she must be hiding something down there. Also, what was that knocking? I have to find out what's happening, but first, I need the key."

After drinking another glass of water, Danny crept to the front room and peeked inside to find his aunt, hunched back in her chair, asleep. He slithered over to the basement door, and taking a deep breath, he clamped his fist tight, his knuckles white from the pressure.

"I have to do this. I have to do this," he quietly repeated to himself, in an attempt to find some courage.

Raising his clenched fist into the air, he thumped on the basement door three times and retreated upstairs as fast as his legs would carry him.

"Who is it? Can't an old lady get some rest?" Aunt Agnes called out in response.

Danny soon heard the familiar shuffling of her pink slippers against the carpet as she dragged herself out of her chair and headed for the front door. She was just about to open it when Danny called out to her.

"I think it came from the basement, Aunt Agnes," Danny informed her.

"Why on Earth would it be coming from there?" She grinned, knowingly, before shuffling back to the front room and seating herself back in her throne. As she sat down, Danny noticed that behind her a large wooden lock box sat central on the mantle.

"Isn't it time you got some work done, pest? Those leaves won't rake themselves," she mumbled almost incoherently, her eyes closed, as she drifted back off to sleep.

Danny didn't dare answer for fear of waking her. Instead he tiptoed forward, his eyes channelled into the lock box on the mantle. Stopping suddenly as something touched his leg, his focus rapidly changed to the obstacle in his path; his aunt's elevated legs. He would need to step over them if he were to get to the box. Sighing, he nervously waved his hand in front of his aunt's face to ensure that she was still asleep. Relieved when she failed to respond, he began stepping over her, one leg at a time. The first was simple; however, with only one hand to help him balance, the second was slightly more difficult, so much so that he nearly fell forwards and landed on his aunt. With both feet planted firmly to the floor and the prize within arm's reach, he leaned forward, looking at it closely for the first time. The box had no key holes or latches; instead there was a puzzle on the lid, requiring pieces to be slid into the correct positions to create an image. Danny couldn't believe his luck, he had never been good at puzzles, but his aunt's laziness had finally worked against her. She had left the puzzle all but complete. With only one piece sitting out of place, he reached over, pushing it gently into the correct position, completing the image of a black cat and causing the box to release a gentle click as the lock became undone. Opening the lid, he instantly noticed that it was empty, except for a single key embedded in the purple velvet lining. Grabbing the key, he gently peeled it away, as he did however, the lid fell shut with a clatter. Danny felt as though he'd been punched in the stomach as the noise echoed off the walls of the room. Aunt Agnes instantly snorted, shuffled across the chair, and continued snoring. Daring to breathe again, Danny leapt over her legs and ran out of the front room before anything else could possibly go wrong.

Outside of the basement he opened out his hand, allowing himself a quick glance at his prize. Reaching over he placed the key gently into the lock.

"Here we go, again," he whispered, before slowly turning it in the hole. The basement door instantly swung open, a gust of wind snatching it in its powerful grip. As he stood atop the wooden steps, unable to see to the bottom, Merelda brushed past his leg and ran down the stairs, black fur camouflaging her into the darkness.

"Merelda, don't go down there. It could be

dangerous," Danny warned, quickly following her down the stairs.

The basement air was thick and damp; a taste of rotten vegetation teasing the back of his throat with every breath. He placed his hand over his nose and mouth in a vain effort to prevent him from gagging. As he reached the basement floor, he felt something cold slither down his face. Jumping back, he grabbed it, filling the room with a dim light. It was the string to turn on the light switch. Through the dull glow he could see that the basement was cluttered with damp boxes, each holding different memories from Aunt Agnes' past. Reaching into one of the many cartons, Danny pulled out a framed photograph of a pristine, young lady smiling at him through the cracked glass. Though the picture was faded with age, he still knew it was a young Aunt Agnes.

"What happened to her? She used to be so happy," he observed, almost sad that he only knew her as the wretched, old lady she had become in her later years.

Placing the photograph carefully back into the box, he turned around to see a large oak workbench fixed firmly to the concrete floor. Moving closer, he quickly recognised the oil lamp that his aunt had been tinkering with earlier. There were no green flames or smoke to be seen this time, however though on closer inspection, there were black wisps within the glass container, each dancing to their own silent song. There was no doubt in his mind; this was definitely Friar's Lantern as his aunt had so abruptly informed him.

"It's beautiful. The way the black pattern moves," Danny said, his eyes darkening the longer he fixated upon it.

Unable to resist the temptation any longer, he scooped it up and held it close to his face, his eyes locked upon the wisps. Danny found himself humming a haunting tune that he didn't recognise as the dance continued.

"Why is that door open?" Aunt Agnes screamed down the stairs.

Startled, Danny leapt backwards, losing his grip on the lantern. As though time itself had slowed, he watched helplessly as it slid from his hand and fell to the floor, glass shattering everywhere. A chilling howl escaped from the remains as the wisps rapidly grew in size and strength, forming a twister within the basement. Bubbling black fluid oozed out and engulfed the broken glass, forming a thick puddle upon the floor.

Darkness filled the room as the wisps grew

stronger, suffocating the light. Their ominous dance came to a sudden halt as they unfolded into their true forms, revealing themselves as shadows, no longer requiring the physical forms of the living to exist. Forming a circle, they surrounded Danny, leaving him frozen to the ground with fear.

"Well, well, well, it looks like you did it for me, pest. You released them," Aunt Agnes laughed maniacally.

"Aunt Agnes. Please, help me," Danny begged as the shadow circle closed in around him. With a disgusting smile, his aunt simple scoffed and turned her back to him.

"It is simply your time, boy, time to enter the shade," she said conclusively.

His options rapidly running out, Danny desperately scanned around the darkening basement for a solution. From across the room, he could see Merelda creeping closer to him through the murkiness.

"No, Merelda. Run. Get out of here," he yelled, trying to chase the cat to safety, but she refused to listen, instead choosing to slink closer.

The shadows closed in on Danny one final time, bearing over him as they slowly reached out to drag him into the eternal shade. Danny fell to his knees, his arms wrapped around his head for protection; he could almost feel the touch of the shadow circle, cold enough to burn. Daring to look up one last time and stare defiantly at his fate, he was stunned to see that the shadows had frozen in place. Down by his feet, Merelda was contently licking up the oozing, black puddle from the lantern. The slender cat's eyes widened, shining a bright emerald green, her mouth sprung open wide, unleashing an almighty screech as the room filled with an explosion of light. Danny's legs shook as he was thrown to the floor, his eyes closed tight, his hands covering his ears desperately trying to block out his senses. He could feel the shadows being torn apart around him but didn't dare to look. Just as suddenly as it had begun, the light dissipated and the room fell into complete silence. Terrified and confused, Danny slowly dared to open one eye to see Merelda had disappeared, and standing proudly in her place was his mother Carolyn.

"Mum? Mum! You? Merelda?" Danny was so stunned that he couldn't find his words.

"Yes, my darling, Tum-Tum. I was Merelda. I was cursed," his mother said, in the reassuring tone that only she was capable of.

"Was it Aunt Agnes? Wait a moment. Where is

Aunt Agnes?" He couldn't see her anywhere.

"That was not your Aunt Agnes," she informed him.

"What? What do you-" Danny jumped back, flinching as a thunderous pounding from across the room interrupted him.

Pulling Danny behind her for safety, his mother slowly crept across the basement toward the constant thudding. As they got closer to the noise, it became clear to Danny that he had heard it before.

"That's the knocking I heard earlier. What is it, Mum?" Danny asked.

As they pushed a pile of old boxes, they tipped. Faded newspapers spread out, carpeting the concrete floor. With a single box remaining in their way, Carolyn pushed it to the side, revealing an old wooden trap door, built into the ground.

"Quick, Danny. Help me open it," she said, removing a jammed crowbar from between the latch and the doors.

Reaching down to grab one of the iron handles, Danny noticed for the first time that his right hand was no longer transparent and had completely returned to normal. He had no time to think about that now though, as he grabbed one of the trapdoors and his mother grabbed the other.

"Pull!" his mother shouted.

Using every ounce of strength they had left, the door creaked angrily as it tore open to reveal an old woman and a young girl, both trapped underground.

"Agnes!" his mother cried out in delight.

"Pip!" Danny called out to his best friend.

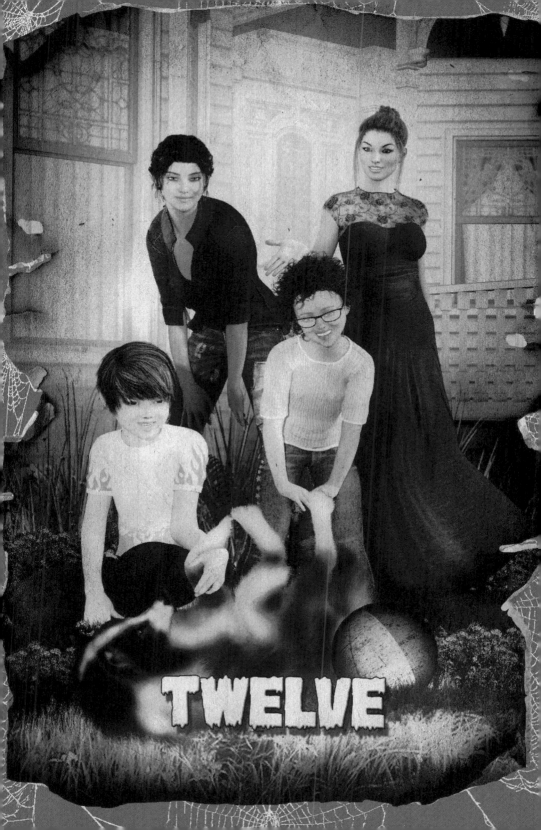

TWELVE

TWELVE

Running back into the basement, Danny returned with a glass of water for his mother, Aunt Agnes, and Pip.

"You must be so thirsty after being locked down there for so long. I'm afraid I could only get water though, Mum. I know cats prefer milk," Danny sniggered.

"Very funny, smarty pants." His mother giggled, wrapping her arm tightly around him and kissing his forehead.

"Actually, I think it may have been an old shelter of some sort, luckily it was all stocked up with bottles of water," Pip told him.

"A-Are you alright, Aunt Agnes?" Danny stuttered.

"Oh, my dear boy, you don't have to fear me. I know they say that first impressions are everything but I assure you that I'm nothing like that horrific creature that posed as me. I promise you, I will make up for every cruel thing you've been through since you arrived here."

Holding her arms out, Danny stepped into a

warm hug from the real Aunt Agnes and the first hug he'd had since he arrived.

"What was that thing that stole your body, Aunt Agnes?" Danny was almost afraid to ask.

"That, my boy, was a Shadow Banshee, an awful creature. With a single scream, they generate the power to steal a small piece of your aura and form a perfect copy of your physical self, but thanks to you, everybody is fine and she has been banished, forever."

"Now, Agnes, I think that's enough scary stories for today, no matter how true they are. What do you say we get out of this miserable basement? I think we've all spent more than enough time down here recently," Danny's mother suggested.

"I think that's a grand idea," Agnes chimed in.

As they headed up the stairs of the basement and into bright light of the kitchen, Danny and Pip were startled by a loud knocking from the front door.

"W-Who is it?" Danny asked, nervously, but was met with an eerie silence.

Nodding to each other, Danny gripped onto

Pip's sleeve for support as they crept toward to the front door. Noticing a switch on the wall, Pip reached over and pushed it, turning on the porch lights. Placing his hand on the cold doorknob, Danny looked over to Pip for approval.

"Do it," she said, nodding to him, once more.

Swinging the door open, Danny looked at the figure before them. Stood in the doorway, in a long beige coat and a brown hat, was the old man from across the street.

"Y-yes?" Danny greeted the figure with as much bravery as he could muster.

The old man stood silently, his cold eyes staring right through Danny and Pip. Glancing past him, Danny noticed that although the porch was well lit, there was no shadow attached to him. Looking back up anxiously, he questioned the old man once again.

"C-can I help you?" Danny just wanted the day to be over.

The wrinkles on the old man's face adjusted, his crooked mouth forming into a smile, as he nodded toward Danny. "I believe this is yours, lad." His raspy voice was now gentle.

A boisterous dog came bounding into the garden, ran through the old man's legs, and jumped at Danny, licking his face frantically.

"Baggles? Baggles!" Danny shouted, unable to contain his excitement.

Crouching down he ruffled Baggles' soft fur as the rambunctious dog ran around in circles, barking excitedly.

Unable to stop smiling, Danny glanced up, desperate to thank the old man for bringing back his best friend, but when he did; the old man was gone, disappeared, without a trace.

Looking from the doorway to each other and back again in utter disbelief, Danny and Pip charged out of the garden and barrelled across the street with Baggles bouncing along behind them. Standing outside of the old man's garden, they read the familiar wooden sign, one last time; 'For Sale'. Gasping, they ran back into Aunt Agnes' house and barged into the kitchen.

"Aunt Agnes, what happened to the old man?" Danny asked, panting.

"What old man, dear?" his aunt replied, curiously.

"The old man from across the street," Danny confirmed.

"Across the street? Honey, that house has been empty for years."

THE END

ABOUT FRANCIS LEGGETT

Born in 1986 on the north-east coast of England, Francis Leggett was always more interested in sports than classroom activities. From a young age he wanted only two things; to become a professional wrestler and to have some written work published. Fifteen years of pro wrestling and a broken body later, Francis is the proud author of the exciting children's horror series Tales of Dark Wonder.

CHECK OUT THE OMP WEBSITE FOR
A COMPLETE LIST OF OUR TITLES

WWW.OPTIMUSMAXIMUSPUBLISHING.COM

BOOKS ARE AVAILABLE IN BOTH PRINT
AND ELECTRONIC FORMATS